## Spot Song

Are you short or tall?
Can you run faster than us all?
Then take a bow
And compete in the Spot Games now.
All sports are good for you.
They keep your spots healthy too!

Is gymnastics your cup of tea?
Do you like to swim in the sea?
Then take a bow
And compete in the Spot Games now.
All sports are good for you.
They keep your spots healthy too!

Do you love to play ping-pong?
Can you jump really long?
Then take a bow
nd compete in the Spot Games now.
All sports are good for you.
hey keep your spots healthy too!

First published in Belgium and Holland by Clavis Uitgeverij, Hasselt – Amsterdam, 2013
Copyright © 2013, Clavis Uitgeverij

English translation from the Dutch by Clavis Publishing Inc. New York
Copyright © 2015 for the English language edition: Clavis Publishing Inc. New York

Visit us on the web at www.clavisbooks.com

*Igor Spot Champion* written and illustrated by Guido van Genechten
Original title: *Igor Stippelkampioen*
Translated from the Dutch by Clavis Publishing

ISBN 978-1-60537-197-9

This book was printed in January 2015 at Wai Man Book Binding (China) Ltd. Flat A, 9/F., Phase 1, Kwun Tong Industrial Centre, 472-484 Kwun Tong Road, Kwun Tong, Kowloon, H.K.

First Edition
10 9 8 7 6 5 4 3 2 1

# Igor
## Spot Champion

Written and illustrated by

Guido van Genechten

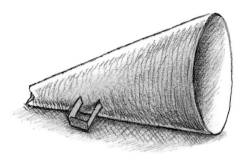

Clavis

**NEW YORK**

The Spot Games are the smallest sports competitions in the world, but for spotted athletes they're the most important ones!

The Games are held every four months.
Between games everyone trains hard.

Athletes run, jump, lift weights, and swim.
Hundreds of push-ups and sit-ups are done.

At last everyone is in top form.
Igor exercises his little vocal cords.

When the time finally comes,
a former champion lights the Spot Fire with a torch.

The chairman of the Spot Committee welcomes everyone.
He says that participation is more important than winning
and wishes all the participants the best of luck.
He ends by saying "LET THE SPOT GAMES BEGIN!"

Sportsmen and sportswomen from all over the world
enter the stadium, cheering.
Igor is competing for the first time.
That's why he walks in front and gets to carry the Spot Flag.

Hup hey

Many sports are part of the Spot Games.
Like high jumping...

...but Igor is still a bit too little for that.

(You need to have really long legs.)

**And Igor knows that to do the long jump you need to jump really far.**
(The Spot Record is a huge 3 ½ inches!)

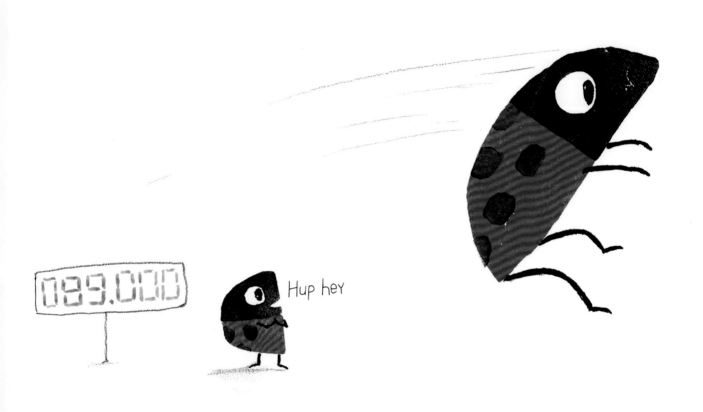

Gymnastics maybe? On the flying rings or the balance beam?
Phew, that's a bit too complicated for Igor.

**All those somersaults and double twists look really difficult!**

Igor does like ping-pong.
But for now the table is still a bit too high for him.

And weights are just too heavy.

0167 GR

Hup
hey

**Maybe later.**
**When he is big and strong.**
(And has done a whole lot of push-ups and sit-ups.)

**Right now, Igor weighs less than an ant and is still a bit small.**

But he is perfect as...

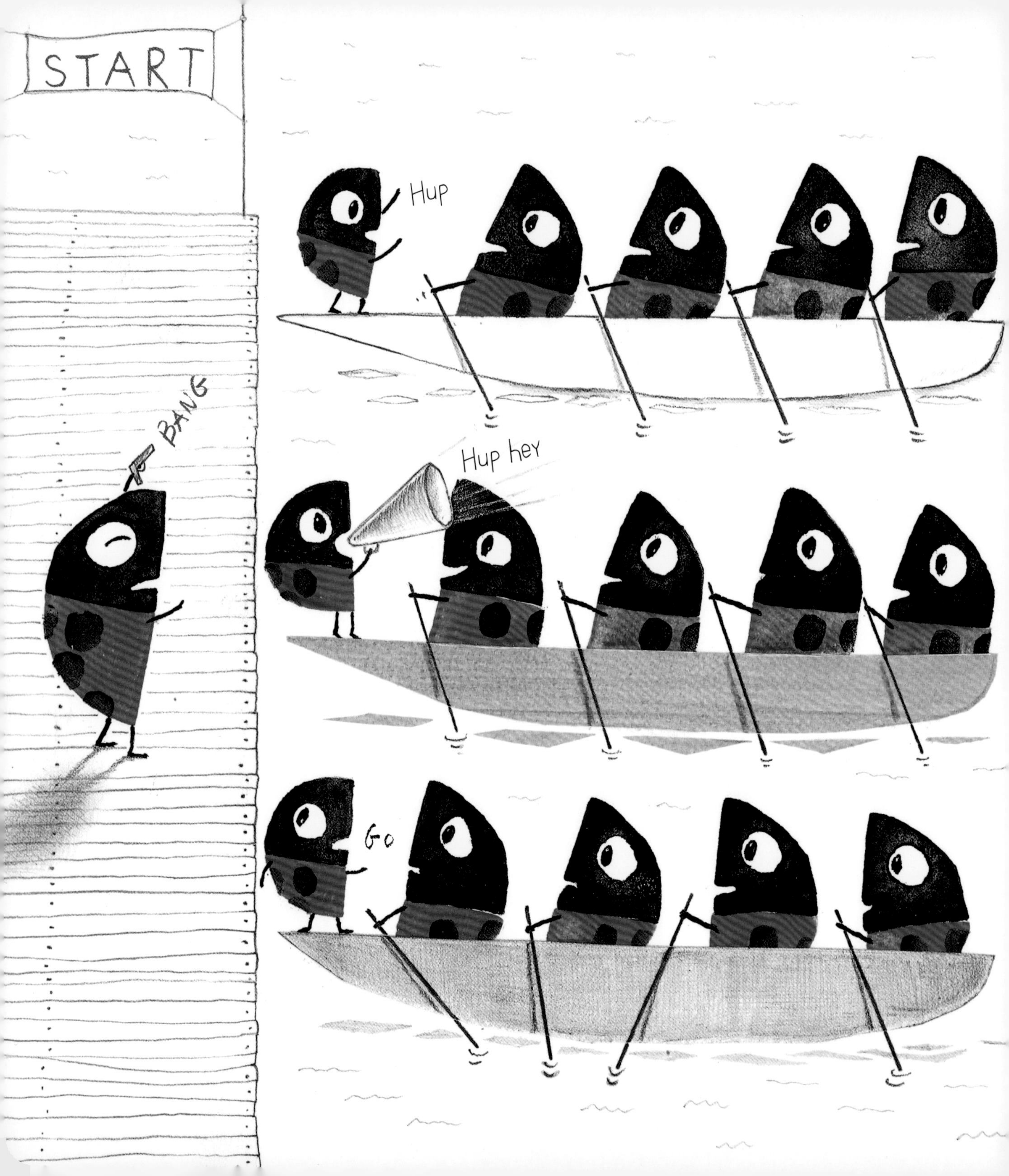
START
BANG
Hup
Hup hey
GO

...the coxswain for the lightweight four.
Igor is steering the red boat. He sets the pace.
Bang! The starting shot sounds.
"Hey...hup, hey...hup!" Igor calls through his megaphone.

"Hey...hup, hey...hup!"
Halfway in the race the white boat is in the lead.
"Hey-hup, hey-hup," Igor calls faster and faster.
"Hey-hup-hey-hup-hey-hup..."
His four rowers row as fast as Igor calls.

And it works! The red boat gets closer and closer.
"Heyhup-heyhup," Igor rouses his rowers for the final stretch.
And, they pass the white boat!
At the very last second, they win the race! Thanks to Igor.

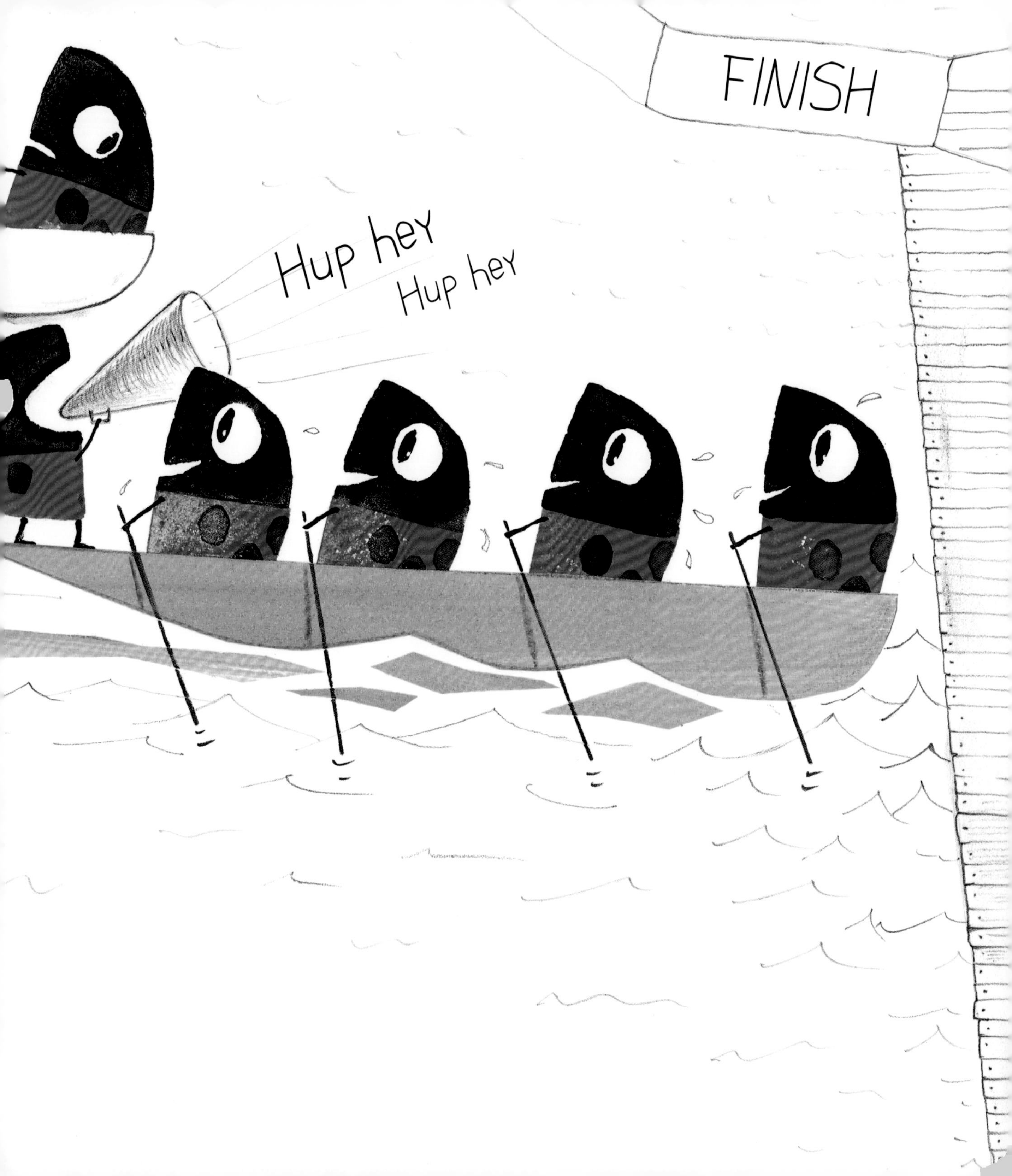
FINISH
Hup hey
Hup hey

At the closing ceremony everyone sings the Spot Song.
Then Igor and all the other athletes receive their medals.
"Participating in the Spot Games is more important than winning,"
the chairman reminds everyone.